Has Anyone Seen CHRISTMAS?

Written by Anne Margaret Lewis

Illustrated by Wendy Popko

Mackinac Island Press

for the love of reading

First Edition

Library of Congress Cataloging-in-Publication Data

Lewis, Anne Margaret and Popko, Wendy
Has Anyone Seen Christmas?
Summary: Emit the Elf must take a journey through every holiday of the year after falling out of Christmas Eve.
He brings all of his holiday friends along with him and learns the true meaning of Christmas.
ISBN 0-9749145-7-6
Fiction

10 9 8 7 6 5 4 3 2

Printed and bound in Canada by Friesens, Altona, Manitoba

A Mackinac Island Press, Inc. publication
www.mackinacislandpress.com

Thank you to my parents for teaching me how to dream;
and thank you to my husband Michael for believing in me.

Wendy Popko

To my children, Caitlin, Matthew, Patrick and Cameron;
and to my husband Brian, who always makes Christmas a special time for our family.

Anne Margaret Lewis

To all the children of the world who believe in the spirit of Christmas!

Mackinac Island Press

Emit (pronounced em-it)
Emit was named after the word "time," spelled backwards. The author wanted to use
this because time is so important to all of us, and can be one of the most precious gifts
we give, not only during the holidays, but all year long!

Each and every Christmas Eve,
Santa flies his sleigh.
He chooses a special North Pole elf,
To help him find his way.

Christmas Eve came quick this year,
And Santa just could not decide;
Which elf would be his navigator?
"You!" he bellowed, winking his eye.

"Emit is my name," I answered in surprise.
"I'll be happy to navigate your sleigh
So all the children on your special list
Will have presents on Christmas Day."

Off we went to deliver presents...
...UP, UP, UP and away...

...the snowstorm made for a bumpy ride,
And bump, bump, bump... *I fell out of Santa's sleigh!*

Down, down, down I went,
Bouncing from cloud to cloud.
Snowflakes slowly changed to confetti;
"HAPPY NEW YEAR!" the crowd shouted aloud.

I was running to find Christmas Day,
When I tripped over Baby New Year;
"Have you seen Christmas?" I asked.
He replied, "No, Emit the Elf, it's not here."

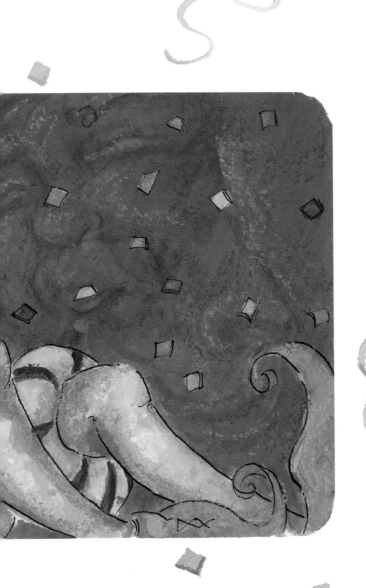

"Has anyone here seen Christmas?
Has anyone seen Christmas Day?
I need to get back to Santa," I cried.
"For I fell out of his sleigh."

As I stumbled out of New Year's Eve,
The confetti became red hearts;
Then cupid shot me with his arrow;
"Ouch!" I yelped, "That's sharp!"

"Have you seen Christmas?"
I asked Cupid of Valentine's Day.
"No, but will you be my valentine?"
He asked, blowing a kiss my way.

"Has anyone here seen Christmas?
Has anyone seen Christmas Day?
I need to get back to Santa," I cried.
"For I fell out of his sleigh."

I wandered out of Valentine red,
It quickly turned to green.
Hundreds of shamrocks sprang from the ground–
More than I had ever seen.

Mr. Leprechaun jumped out of nowhere.
"Hello wee little Emit the Elf!"
"Have you seen Christmas?" I asked.
"Noooo," he replied, "I haven't
    seen it meself."

"Has anyone here seen Christmas?
Has anyone seen Christmas Day?
I need to get back to Santa," I cried.
"For I fell out of his sleigh."

Off we marched, Mr. Leprechaun and I,
Leaving hundreds of shamrocks behind.
The road began to swirl and swell
With rainbow colors...2...no 5...no 9!

Green and red, and orange and yellow;
Purple, pink and blue;
Twisting and turning like Santa does,
Down the chimney flue.

With a whirr and a crash
We flew off the rainbow slide,
Right into the Easter factory,
My holiday friends and I.

I bumped into the Easter Bunny,
Hopping on his pogo stick;
"Have you seen Christmas?" I asked.
He gave a quick "No!" with a clickety-click.

"Has anyone here seen Christmas?
Has anyone seen Christmas Day?
I need to get back to Santa," I cried.
"For I fell out of his sleigh."

We continued on our journey,
With Easter eggs in tow;
Birthday balloons were everywhere
"Make a wish," I yelled—"Now, blow!"

"Have you seen Christmas?"
I asked the birthday girl as she looked at me.
"No, but I have some birthday cake;
Would you like to have a piece? It's free."

"Has anyone here seen Christmas?
Has anyone seen Christmas Day?
I need to get back to Santa," I cried.
"For I fell out of his sleigh."

We left the birthday party,
Then found a giant balloon.
"All aboard my holiday friends!
Come on, Easter Bunny...you, too."

Up, up, up and away we rose,
Balloons bursting on Lady Liberty's crown.
With a pop and a crack and a deafening boom,
Our hot air balloon was sent down.

Lady Liberty stood there before us
With John Hancock and Ben Franklin, too.
"Have you seen Christmas?" I asked her,
With her face a green shade of blue.

"No, Emit the Elf," she replied,
As she held up her stately flame.
"Perhaps you should board the pumpkin coach
And check out some Halloween games."

"Has anyone here seen Christmas?
Has anyone seen Christmas Day?
I need to get back to Santa," I cried.
"For I fell out of his sleigh."

We charged on our way in this pumpkin-like sleigh,
Leaving 4th of July fast behind.
Down we went, using Trick-or-Treat Lane,
Following the Halloween sign.

"Have you seen Christmas?"
I yelled to the costumed boy crossing the street.
"No Emit, I'm afraid it's simply not here!"
Then he bellowed aloud, "TRICK-OR-TREAT!"

"Has anyone here seen Christmas?
Has anyone seen Christmas Day?
I need to get back to Santa," I cried.
"For I fell out of his sleigh."

March two...three...four,
To Christmas we will go;
Pumpkins became plump turkeys,
Pilgrims and Indians gave a gleeful hi-ho.

The Thanksgiving Day Parade marched on,
With all of my holiday friends.
"Santa must be here somewhere!" I screamed;
"Does this Thanksgiving Parade ever end?"

"Have you seen Christmas?"
I asked Mr. Turkey, leading the parade so proud.
"No Emit!" he shouted with all the commotion,
And the bass drum beating so loud.

"Has anyone here seen Christmas?
Has anyone seen Christmas Day?
I need to get back to Santa," I cried.
"For I fell out of his sleigh."

"Christmas is right around the corner!"
Mr. Turkey gobbled and grinned.
"And I thought I saw the great Santa Claus,
He's in the Parade...at the end."

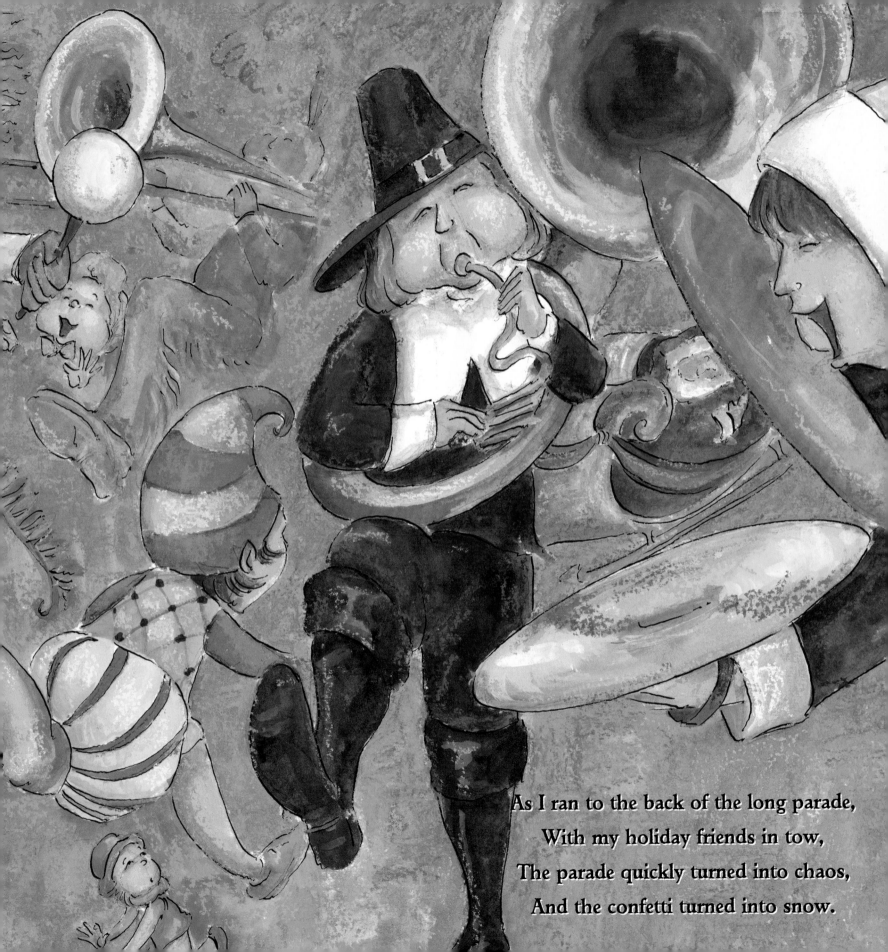

As I ran to the back of the long parade,
With my holiday friends in tow,
The parade quickly turned into chaos,
And the confetti turned into snow.

The noise of the drums
Could no longer be heard;
The night became quite silent—
Not a peep...not a sound...
...not a word!

A young boy grabbed my hand.
"Come on Emit, come follow me,
I've seen Christmas right here;
It's in my house, with my tree."

The boy and his sister ran quickly inside
In a flash, in a blink of the eye.
They paused at the door to invite us all in—
My holiday friends and I.

The boy watched as we all marched in,
With many gifts for all to see.
Not just Easter eggs, birthday cake and
    valentine cards,
But joy and hope and peace.

"Christmas is here Emit,"
The boy said with a sigh.
He stood by the tree with joy on his face,
And a grateful tear in his eye.

Now I was back to Christmas,
And there appeared Santa's sleigh,
With Santa standing there beside it,
Winking, happy I had found my way.

Santa bent down and looked in my eyes.

"Emit, it's not only gifts I deliver.

It's friendship, family and Christmas spirit,"

He said quietly with a quick little quiver.

Merry Christmas

"Come now Emit," Santa said sweetly,
"Come my little time-traveling friend.
Let all of your holiday friends know
It's a message of goodness I send."